Son, You Are A King

By Tená V. Baker

Illustrated by Jasmine Hatcher

To my husband, Nicholas and my mother, Valentina who have continually lifted and loved me in spite of me. I love you.

Summary: What does a young boy do when faced with bullying, loneliness, and fear?
This is the story of a boy losing his innocence and finding his power.

Presented To:_____

From:_____

Today was pretty hard. Between the teasing and doubting myself, sometimes it's hard to do my best. I just don't understand why they don't like me.

Pick your head up, son.
You are a king.

I don't always have the nicest things, but I like the way I look.

Pick your head up, son.
You are a king.

I'm always the first they pick to play ball, but never for the group projects.

Pick your head up, son. You are a king.

I told my friend I want to be an engineer. He told me to stick to basketball. "How many engineers on TV look like you?"

Pick your head up, son.
You are a king.

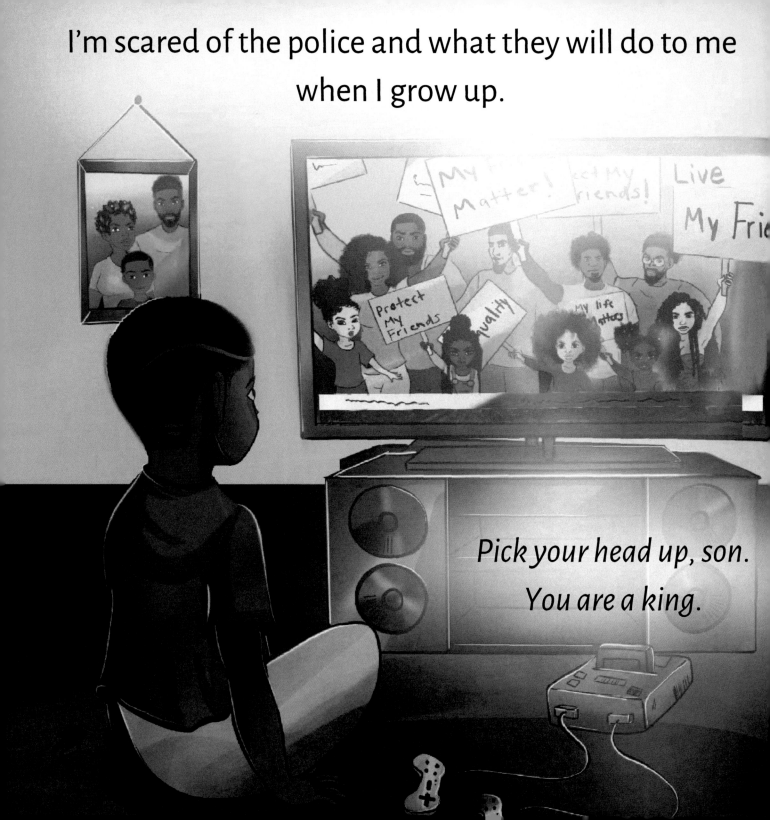

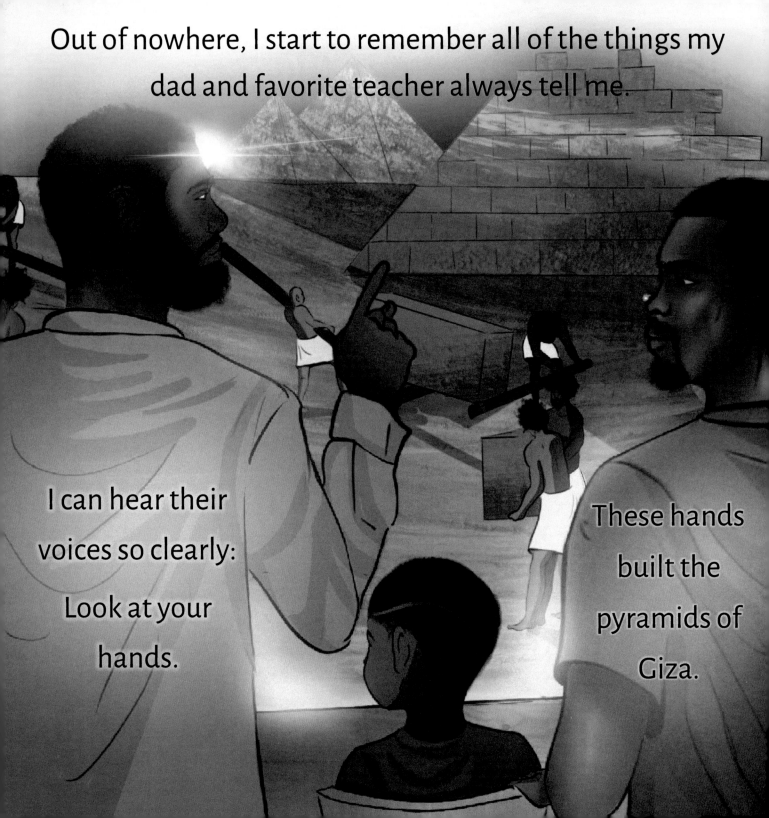

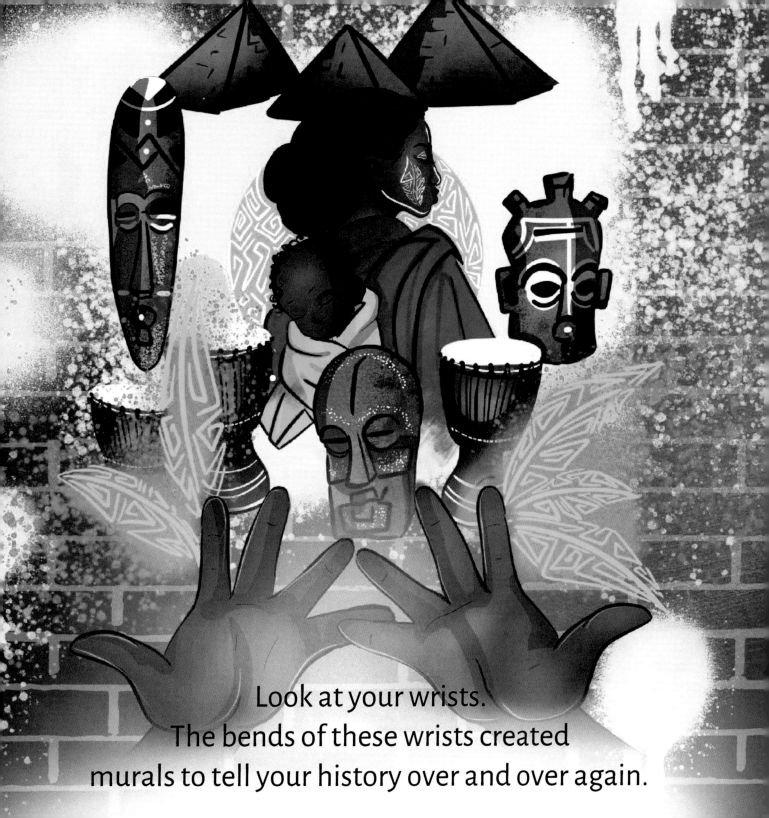

Look at your wrists.
The bends of these wrists created
murals to tell your history over and over again.

Look at your feet.

These feet ran hundreds of miles to discover new land.

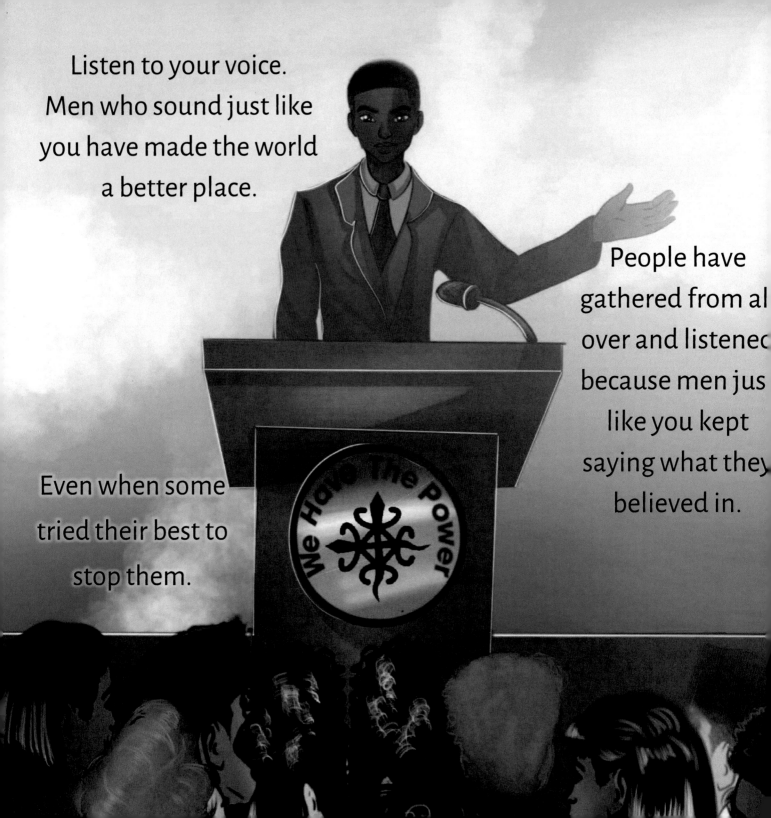

Your mind is the founder of arithmetic and science.

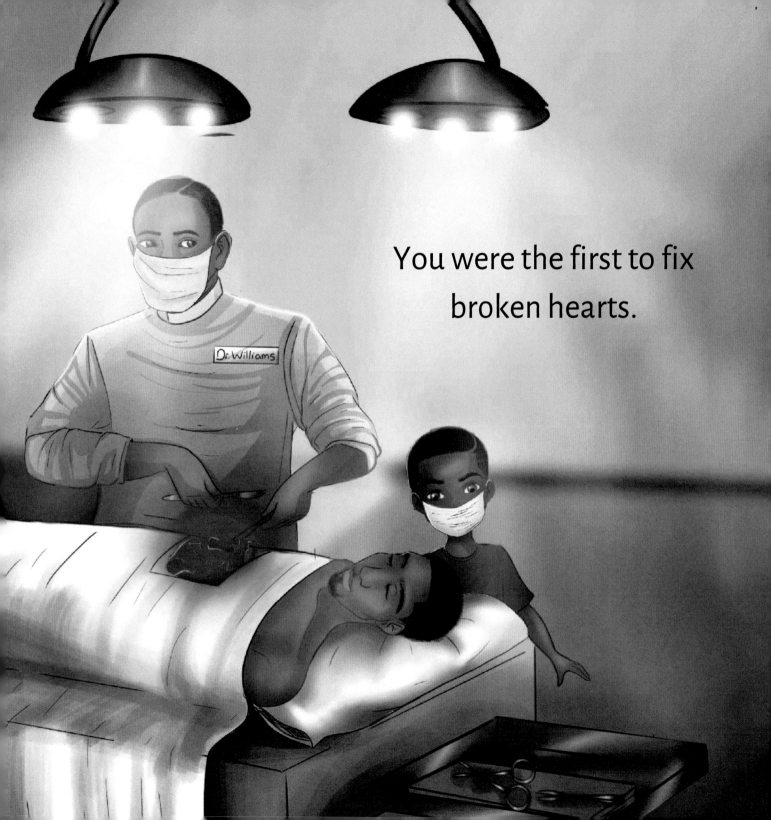

You were the first to fix broken hearts.

You created methods to grow crops in dry places to feed your family.

The mastery of your mind does not need a map to find its way.

So, before you drift to sleep tonight
pray a simple prayer that tomorrow
you will know how great you are
and the rest of the world will meet
you there.

Keep your head up, son.

You are a king.

ABOUT THE AUTHOR

Tená grew up a small-town girl from Warsaw, VA with huge dreams. As an alumna of Howard University, she soon became an advocate for justice and social change. For many years she kept her gift of writing very personal, using it primarily as an outlet to express her own tears of trials and triumphs. However, seeing the need to create change from the inside out in an unrelenting society, she felt purposed to write this premier piece of Even Me Empowerment to empower children and adults alike to not only be resilient but to heal. Visit www.evenmeempowerment.com to learn more about the author, schedule bookings, and grab free resources.

Dear Reader: (A Word from the Author)

Thank you for reading Son, You Are A King. Please take a moment and leave a review on www.amazon.com. We would love to hear how this book empowered you and your little one.

Be on the lookout for the sister book coming soon!

Made in the USA
Monee, IL
30 March 2021